The Word is SMUT

First published in 2024 by Cambridge Writing Centre

Compiled and Edited by
        Sarah Kenner (Lead Editor)
        Rachel Varnham
        Lillie Weston

Proofread by
        Jac Harmon
        Sarah Kenner
        Freya Sacksen
        Lisa Sargeant
        Rachel Varnham

Cover Design by
        Sarah Kenner

With special thanks to Jon Stone for his support and
guidance throughout.

ISBN: 978-1-909560-37-6

An Introduction to The Word is

The Word is aims to be a place for playful creativity centred around the multifaceted nature of a single word, where Anglia Ruskin students (past and present) can showcase written and visual work that is of a high calibre, thematically appropriate and compelling. We want to make a space for the diverse voices of our community to experiment and express themselves through the joy of artistic creation. All the pieces within are tied together by their connection to at least one of the multiple definitions of "smut".

We hope you enjoy this first collection as much as we do, and that you allow it to pull you along the many varied interpretations the word smut has inspired in our contributors whether steamy, gut-wrenching, playful, powerful, unexpected or just plain smutty.

The Word is:
SMUT

smut

/smʌt/

noun

noun: smut; plural noun: smuts

> 1. a small flake of soot or other dirt or a mark left by one.
> "all those black smuts from the engine"

> 2. a fungal disease of cereals in which parts of the ear change to black powder.
> "a few bad crop years with smut and drought and frost"

> 3. obscene or lascivious talk, writing, or pictures.
> "porn, in his view, is far from being harmless smut"

Origin is from the German 'schmutzen' to 'smut' inlate Middle English (in the sense 'defile, corrupt, make obscene'); compare with smudge. The noun dates from the mid 17th century.

Contents

Citrus
Sarah Kenner

Vintage Lovers
Jac Harmon

They have not met in person. Onscreen he finds the gap between her front teeth sexy. She adores the magpie-wing sheen of his hair. Over two weeks they discover a shared liking for indie coffee shops, and the work of Kubrick.

He suggests they meet.

She suggests a place.

They agree to dress in outfits expressing their personalities.

His nerves are as tight as the loafers he keeps for special occasions.

She hates her feet, and longs for petite size fives as she pulls on her socks.

He waits in a booth. When he gets up to greet her a spark of electricity crackles between her poodle skirt and his nineteen-fifties peg trousers.

They sit side by side luxuriating in each other's touch. The poodle skirt, filled to capacity by layers of netting, hides their ardour from inquisitive eyes.

Heat of thigh on thigh
Cappuccino froths
He fingers petticoat lace

The Nectarine

Freya Sacksen

My boyfriend watches
As I eat slightly
Overripe nectarines
The juice spilling
Like monsoon rain over
My lips and teeth and fingers;

My mouth contorts
In odd shapes around its flesh,
My tongue and teeth
By turns
Sharp and soft against its core;

The purplepinkred skin is
Pulled and strains
Against my pink lips
And he watches.

When I am done,
Lips and fingers wet,
He kisses every finger,
Staining his own mouth;

Then,
Ignoring propriety,
Kisses me deeply,
And tastes of salt.

The Biter
Mia Humphreys

I flopped back onto Clem's pink bedspread while she rooted around in the wardrobe, pulling out an old Reebok backpack. She sat down and withdrew a Tupperware box and a rolling tray.

'I decided on a colour scheme for our flat.'

That was the topic we always returned to, the mythical flat we would share once we finished sixth form. The one we spent long hours working at Asda and Pizza Hut respectively to save for.

The thought made my stomach turn. I still hadn't told her that I had received an unconditional offer for an Undergraduate English degree in Brighton. Clem barely scraped a C in our Summer mocks. The moniker of being Clem's Best Friend had acted as a comfort blanket for most of my life and the thought of throwing it off frightened me, though it sent a little thrill of excitement down my spine too.

'Oh yeah?'

'I'm thinking white and grey. Very minimalist, like the Kardashians.'

She set about rolling us a blunt with her thin fingers. Black hair hung around her head like a dark cloud.

'Also, it'll go great with all the IKEA furniture.'

'Uh huh.'

She opened the window, and sitting on the nook we took turns standing on our knees and blowing the evidence into the crisp Autumn air. I doubt it did much to disguise the overwhelming smell that clung to everything. Clem would recall with much delight the rare occasions where her parents would challenge her on her habit. She would laugh recounting where they could stick their rules.

Clem was wild in that way. It reminded me a bit of my nan's dog, this fat little bastard of a Jack Russell who would bark non-stop whenever the doorbell rang. They never took him to dog training so when he pinched a spare sock or pen that was dropped on the floor, they'd give him a treat instead of fighting him for it.

'You'll never guess who didn't text me "good morning" today.'

'The Pope?'

She gave me a look with one eyebrow raised that made her look particularly haughty and beautiful. Her eyelids were painted purple with eyeshadow, like a bruise. It was Alex, of course.

I didn't have a problem with Alex, per se. He was nice enough on his own. I could see how his long hair and wardrobe of second-hand jumpers might be appealing to some. But I hated him on principle for the sheer number

13

of times she had run back into his skinny arms, especially after I had spent hours consoling her after their break ups.

'Why don't you text him first then?'

Her blue eyes studied my own. She had this habit of looking in other people's eyes to see her own reflection, which gave the odd impression she was staring right past you.

'That's not the point. The point is that if he doesn't text me first then we wouldn't talk.'

'But if you text him first, then you can talk.'

She let out a frustrated sigh that screamed, *ugh, you just don't get it*, and a sudden wave of red-hot hate washed over me.

'Do you think I should break up with him?'

If they broke up, I had a good few weeks of crying and non-stop mentions of he-who-must-not-be-named ahead of me. But then again, if they did break up, I wouldn't have plans cancelled on me at the last minute. I would have Clem all to myself.

'Yeah, could do.'

I fell back on the bed, head swimming while Clem smoked the rest. Once she was done, she threw the roach out of the window and joined me so that we were lying on our backs, side by side.

She bit me playfully on the shoulder, not hard enough to hurt but hard enough to feel the indents of her teeth. Incisors, canines, and a hint of premolars. It was her own funny way of showing affection.

I wondered if Alex bit too. What would they do then? There couldn't be two biters in the relationship. It was one or the other, the biter and the bitten.

'I'm gonna get a drink. You want some?'

I nodded, my eyes never leaving the ceiling. The cream walls were spiked with little paint mountains – ready to poke anyone who came close enough. Another thing crossed my vision, a bottle of red wine. I sat up.

'Guess what I found in the garage.' Clem held it aloft, a triumphant smile spread across her face. Her teeth were as straight and white as a military cemetery.

I took it in my hands, turning it over as I read the label. '2000…' I looked up at her.

'This is the expensive shit.'

'I know.'

'This is older than us.'

'Yeah, because it's been gathering dust in the garage. I bet they've forgotten it's even back there.'

'Or maybe they're saving it for a special occasion.'

'Stop being so boring and help me open it.'

After a few passes with a corkscrew and then a butter knife, we managed to get the bottle open. Clem took a swig, screwing up her nose as she did so.

She handed it back to me and I revelled in the warmth that spread across my chest. It tasted a lot better than the stolen liquor I was used to. The lukewarm Malibu we drank in the fields near the sixth form.

We passed the bottle back and forth, becoming slowly more fucked up until the streetlights turned on outside.

I sat back against the headboard while Clem painted my nails, then toenails like I was her own oversized doll. While she painted, I inspected the bottle. It read in small print: '*Ravish me Red.*'

Getting bored, I wiggled my toes ever so slightly.

'Stop! You're messing them up!' She squealed and I couldn't help but wonder if she ever made those noises for Alex.

'Oh, I just remembered, I bought rave tickets with Alex.' The words came out slow and slurred. She ran a hand through her hair and groaned dramatically.

'I can't break up with him until January 17th...'

I just sat there and let Clem talk at me. She was one of those people who could talk for hours, even if she didn't know you from Adam. If you stood still long enough, she'd tell you everything about her.

I hated that. I hated that everything she told me in hush conspiratorial tones was the same bullshit she told everyone else. The personal details she shared that would make you feel so special were as easy conversation topics as the weather.

She finished up and joined me back on the bed. 'Now don't move for another ten minutes.'

We sat in silence, listening to music. The drumbeat was as real and visceral as a heartbeat. I turned my head and bit down on her shoulder, gently. The knit of her jumper felt weird on my tongue. I withdrew slightly, and closed my mouth so that it became a clothed kiss. I moved up until my lips were on her neck, soft and light as a feather. Her breathing was quite still, though I could feel her pulse fluttering in her neck like a trapped butterfly. She may have let out a nervous chuckle. Maybe she asked what I was doing. It was as though the world fell away and all I saw was the pale skin of her neck.

I opened my mouth and bit. A lover's bite. I pulled the milky skin between my teeth and sucked. She gasped softly.

'What are you doing?' Her voice was low and breathy, almost a moan. I could feel her ribs expand under her jumper like a shocked animal. Her back arched ever so slightly.

Not big enough of a deal to tell her boyfriend. We got too fucked, that's it. And besides all girls do it at sleepovers. Come morning, we would forget. Life would go on like normal.

I bit down, hard.

Clay Boobs

Jac Harmon

Clay

Boobs

Handmade

Unbalanced

No body's perfect

But every body is unique

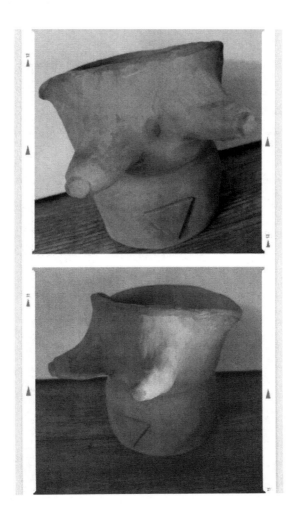

21

Afternoon Delight
at the Florist
Sarah Kenner

As a splash of milk is not adequate protection against
the heat of boiling water, Red scalded her mouth on the
first sip of instant coffee. She rolled her tongue to take
out some of the sting, then having seemingly learned
nothing she took another painful sip before leaving the still
full cup behind on the counter where it would cool to a
comfortable temperature without anyone around to drink
it.

The door slammed locked behind her as she rushed
down her street towards the station. She was in a hurry,
meeting her mother for lunch so they could have another
one-sided conversation.

The day had seemed to be warming, so she had left
the house without a proper jacket, opting for a red knitted
shawl instead. Probably not smart for mid-November,
where a chill could pick up without a moment's notice, but
done was done, Red reasoned, and as she was already on
the Piccadilly line, it was much too late to go back for a
jacket now.

Standing in a crowd of overly perfumed strangers all
avoiding eye contact, Red made a mental game of guessing
which of her mother's many disappointments would

feature first on their conversational agenda: How she was a neglectful daughter, who didn't spend enough time with her mother. How upsetting it was that Red still hadn't gone back to finish her degree and was instead wasting her life at a bakery. How, at twenty-eight, the clock was really running out on those darling little grandchildren her mother wanted.

A taste of blood gave Red pause. In her frustration she had worried her lip to bleeding. She let out a sigh, pushing the thoughts away; no point taking on the sorrows of the day before they arrived. Red joined the throng getting off at Covent Garden Station, before walking at a brisk pace down a side street, in an attempt to find just a moment of breathing room.

That's when she saw it, the flower shop: a brick building taller than it was wide, with dark green panelling at the bottom; it shared walls with a haberdashery on one side and a used bookshop on the other.

She couldn't say what had made her stop. There wasn't time for it; she was already awfully late. But somehow her feet carried her to the stained glass door anyway.

The image on it was a breathtaking tableau of a winter forest under a full moon, two figures moving through the trees, one draped in red cloth, the other naked and with the head of a wolf. Next to the door was a sign *Perrault's Pins and Needles, Flower Emporium*. A quick peek inside probably couldn't hurt.

Stepping through the door, the first thing Red noticed was the moisture-rich air, and the scent of living green things that clung to everything; a mixture of moss and florals. The second thing she noticed was a man standing with his back to her. Or rather, she noticed the way his washed-out blue jeans seemed to perfectly sculpt his bum. Red allowed herself a moment to devour him with her eyes, enjoying the way his shop logo t-shirt hung loosely off his wide-shouldered frame, and the tousled look of his short brown hair. Then he turned, and she busied her eyes with hanging flower pots, and buckets stuffed with an assortment of brightly coloured flowers.

'Welcome to *Pins and Needles*, your path to the perfect floral experience.'

He managed the greeting in one exhale. Then, as her eyes met his, he stepped forward, a smile pulling at the edge of his lips.

'I'm Wulff, how can I help you today?'

'Oh, just browsing,' she sounded breathy, even to her own ears.

'We've got some beautiful peonies in, just begging for someone to take them home in a bouquet. Or are you more of a houseplant kind of woman? 'Cause we have a lovely selection of succulents in the back.'

'I don't know.'

'Shall I leave you to it then? Just give a shout if you need me.'

He lingered a moment, a hand at the back of his neck, before turning away.

'Wait. What's this one?' Red asked, mostly to keep him talking, while pointing vaguely to her right, at a large potted plant. It was a delicate thing made up of twisting leafy vines, and a scattering of big purple flowers, supported by a wooden trellis. He let one finger graze across the soft fold of a petal, before answering,

'Clitoria, also known as butterfly pea.'

'And that one?'

She stepped closer to him as she spoke, gesturing to a collection of tiny yellow trumpet-like flowers on long stems in a pot hanging by his shoulder. He turned to follow her gesture, brushing his body against hers in the process.

'That's honeysuckle. It has a really nice scent.'

He lifts one of the blooms; an invitation. She leans down, pressing her face against it, closing her eyes, she breathes in. A cascade of floral scents wash through her, sending a tingle down her spine. She straightens, only to become acutely aware of how very close their bodies are. She lifts her eyes, finding his, she reaches one hand towards his chest, not quite touching, her nose still filled with the subtle perfume of honeysuckle sweetness. A moment. A pause. A leaning into each other until hands touch bodies and lips meet. The soft, uncertain, question quickly answered with grasping hands and shattering need. A scratch of stubble against the pout of a lower lip. He pulls away, his eyes on her mouth as he speaks:

'I'm going to lock the door, don't move. Please.'

This is it. The moment for Red to regain her senses. To stop before things go any further. She feels the red shawl glide off her shoulder, and lets it fall. He is watching her. His gaze, penetrating, as he stalks across the floor. Devour. She walks to him.

> Body begs to lap up honeysuckle with a twist of tongue.
> Puckered petals drawn through tips of hungry teeth, call out calla-lily.
> Ranunculus crushed beneath groping hands, soft hues of red scattered across tender skin.
> The tingle of a tickle of fine hairs.
> Strands of lavender bound in thread dance across the swell of an eager throat.
> Knees bruise fallen honeysuckle, as fingernails leave

red marks across thick daisy white thighs.

Fingers graze the soft folds of a dahlia.

Fumble across slick skin.

Succulents, leaves light green with pink tips, are thick to bursting, moisture leaking out with one soft squeeze.

Purple-hued clitoria, curved to invite caressing butterfly kisses.

Sticky residue, clinging nectar, sweet viscous secretion.

Red felt pretty sure a flower petal had made its way into her panties, there was definitely decorative moss in her hair, and any chance she had of making her appointment on time was long gone. But it had been worth it. His smile was bright and dimpled, his eyes never straying from her face, as he walked beside her to the door. Pulling it open, they were met with a rush of cold air, freckled with snow. Red groaned, feeling fully unprepared to return to the world outside.

'Wait. Don't go anywhere. I'll be right back,' Wulff said.

Red closed the door, wanting to keep the heat in as she waited, taking in with equal measure embarrassment and satisfaction the state their tumble had left the flower shop in. Greenery of all kinds lay scattered across the floor, a pot had been knocked over, spilling dirt, and the moisture-rich air, with its floral earthy scent, had an undertone of sweat and secretions that Red found tantalising. Just as tantalising as she found the man returning to her with a fur-lined coat slung over one arm.

'Here, take this,' he said, handing it to her.

'You're giving me your coat?'

'No, I'm lending it to you. You can give it back to me when you meet me for drinks Friday night. Around 8, at Grandma's Blind Tiger, the pub down the street?'

'Okay, I'll see you then. Thanks.'

She put on his fur-lined coat, pulling her red shawl around her neck like a scarf. Then she offered Wulff one last quick kiss before opening the door. Red made her way to her mother, strolling through the streets with her head held high and a smile pulling at her cheeks, as flakes of frost settled in her hair.

Crows
Dan Leighton

between sky and soil
hovering in the liminal
arcs of time jittered

moments fluttering
charcoal smeared points
juddering in the blue

croaking flights casting
shining sable pinions
creaking in the wind

untrusted earth observed
by blackened beads
swivelling in the sky

Roadkill
Candy Smellie

Barry realises that at the age of 50 he's probably among the oldest in the pack, but in full furry fursona, they'll only know him as Badger. The striking black body and luminescent white stripe down the back is perhaps one of the best furry costumes he's ever seen. It cost a fortune, something Maureen's not aware of, but so worth it.

He loves Maureen. Theirs is not a loveless marriage. Yes, it's been more than 20 years since they've had sex but that doesn't mean he doesn't love her. He's aware that she's been responsible for her own orgasms for most of their marriage, but she seems alright with that. She has a room of her own where she keeps her favourite books and a TV with access to all the Netflix and Prime shows she likes to watch. She protects it fiercely. Barry struggles with the Sky box on the 'big' TV so generally watches reruns of old sitcoms and episodes of 'Escape to the Country'. He moves quietly around the house so as not to disturb her, knowing this is what she would want.

He told Maureen months ago that he'd been thinking of joining the furry community and though she wasn't fully behind the idea, she was at least prepared to drive him to the meetings. Even if it is a little awkward, he believes she's pleased he has found a hobby that gets him out of the house.

Barry's very new to this world. Despite the furtive nature of furries dressing in their other skins, he has found others to take advice from. He has his new fursona all prepared and now can't wait to introduce Badger to the others. And of course, there's his chance to finally meet 'Susie'. She is also a badger. He's talked to her online and they have agreed to meet at the hotel this weekend. He can't wait. He doesn't feel as if he is being unfaithful to Maureen, even if Susie has something further on her mind when they do finally unite. He hasn't told her his real name, they have only exchanged short video calls as badgers, so he has no idea what she looks like, or even how old she is. But he has found her little yips and snuffles delightful.

He packs a huge bag, so big that it's almost impossible to get the zip closed on the fake fur, and drags it bumping down the stairs. He looks into the sitting room where Maureen is waiting, sullen, silently judging but acquiescing, car keys in her handbag. She reluctantly rises from the sofa, preparing to drive him to the motel in the next town. He knows that she told her friends he was in the local Am Dram production of Wind in the Willows, and this is the ruse they will use if any of her girlfriends spot him in his alternate Badger.

Barry is sitting quietly in the passenger seat, trying to remain calm even though Maureen's excessive speed is making him uncomfortable. He glances at her; her silence feels punitive. They are taking side roads to avoid meeting anyone they know. Even though it's late summer the lanes are dark; huge branches of the nearest trees overhang the tarmac creating tunnel-like byways.

Maureen throws the car round a corner, nearly knocking a cyclist into the hedgerow. These lanes are not so quiet after all. There is horror just visible on the opposite verge. Smeared around the ditch to their left is a mess of bones, gristle and skin, the deer clearly dead and probably has been for some time. Large crows are making a meal of the carcass, though there is little of the meat remaining. It turns Barry's stomach, already full of nerves for the coming event. Maureen slows slightly, scattering the corvids but avoids driving over the body. Barry manages a good look at the corpse and really wished he hadn't.

Arriving at the Travelodge, Maureen pulls up to the front of the hotel and Barry jumps out, retrieving the bag from the boot. He waves her off, saying see you Sunday. He raises an arm in farewell, but can't tell if she's seen him, so fast did she disappear down towards the road.

It is time for Barry to become Badger and don his other skin. The one he feels most comfortable in. The one he's been biding his time to wear. No underwear this weekend, he's going commando. The thought alone gives Barry mild sexual pleasure. Something he's not experienced for years.

He looks at his reflection as best he can in the mirror and even there, in the bad light of the bedroom, he is pleased with the results. The sheen of the white on black fur sparkles. Viewed from inside the mask's plastic eyelets, he knows he looks impressive.

Time to go out and meet his new pack mates. In a satchel swinging from his back are sandwiches and a thermos of hot tea – comforts that he's not prepared to go without. He'd been told there will be some sort of 'appropriate' feast later, but as a fussy eater he isn't willing to take the risk. What if he is expected to eat worms or beetles?

The pack has reserved the function rooms attached to the hotel for their meet and greet. As Badger enters via the lobby, there seems to be some sort of meeting and greeting ritual being performed that he hadn't been prepared for. Around the outside of the room is a collection of straight-backed, metal framed chairs, covered in dark blue brushed nylon. Within this arena, two wolves are circling, the occasional snarl and bark muffled by the impressive heads each are wearing. There are others sniffing around the couple, each eager to join in. The wolves are on all fours but with a strange gait defined by the longer legs and shorter arms of the committed furries. After a while, though Badger hasn't detected any obvious signal, they all sit on their haunches, back slapping and laughing, clearly having a great time.

Desperately looking for Susie, he can't see another badger in the room. Just as he is thinking he might leave, a wolf approaches him, welcoming paw outstretched in greeting. Badger allows himself to be drawn into the room where muffled 'hellos' are exchanged. Some remark how good his fursona is, others want to stroke him, and as a good brock, he lets them.

The others are quite a mixed bag. There are woodland animals, foxes, rabbits, even one bear. In the main though, most are either wolves or large dogs. He'd not realised that wolves were so popular, but he supposes that means there is every chance the dinner will more likely be meat based than one suited to the insectivores. Not everyone has on the full head fursona, there are some with just a face mask and a couple with extravagant painted visages. It's all so exciting. But, there is still no sign of Susie. Clearly, she is yet to arrive. To pass the time, Badger starts drinking. This is managed via a straw. They all carry one otherwise no one can drink. Eating is relatively simple and the buffet proved mostly beige, just the way he likes it.

Susie is late and it is after 10pm before she appears. Badger has been drinking quite heavily by then (Dutch courage he calls it) so is feeling a little unsteady when his badger mate finally appears.

'Susie' turns out to be a 6ft ex-marine. He is indeed a badger but not the sort Barry had in mind. Phoning Maureen doesn't go well either. She refuses to come and collect him. Her book group is round for wine and snacks, and she's already had too much to drink to drive, which leaves him no alternative but to walk.

His disappointment is the cloak he wears to bolster him a mile or so towards home, but it's dark now and he's so tired. Nothing for it, he thinks, I'll make like the badger I want to be and build myself a sett, here in the leaves on the side of the road.

Sometime later, in the mist of an early dawn, he begins to feel that perhaps some of his life's choices were not all that they should have been. He is vaguely aware of loud music but can't quite work out what or where it's coming from. In his nest of leaf litter and moss, he feels nothing when the van runs over him.

Mr Right Now –
September Edition
Emma Lister

Friday 1st September 2018

Eric. Sculpted biceps. Fit. His jeans perfectly moulded around his arse cheeks. I felt his interest, a hookup, that's all I desire. Aroused in the throb of the nightclub, seduced by the thumping beat. We found a darkened corner. Hammered on vodka, I allowed kisses and tits. His nose behind my ear, he told me what he wanted. Cringe. Lager-breathed mutterings about my wet pussy made me dry. His designer stubble irritated me. He twiddled my nipple, I grew bored. *You know you want this.* I really didn't.

He had no condom anyway, not wasting mine.

Friday 8th September 2018

Mike, I think. A bad decision in a shitshow of a night. I stank of sick, having already vomited and could hardly stand. Broke a heel strap in a messy fall. The fluorescent lights of the toilets highlighted his flaws: ill-fitting Coldplay t-shirt, massive sweat patches, and bits of gristle in his teeth. It was a relief to turn my back, best to not see it coming. Squashed against the cubicle wall, face pressed into God knows what, while he thrusted and groaned.

He slapped my arse when he was done. Disappointing, I wriggled my skirt back into place and binned my shredded tights.

Bare legs and less alcohol next week.

Friday 15th September 2018

Jimmy. 19. Too young for me. Little brother of a guy I dated last year. Same eyes, but otherwise an upgraded version. Nicer hair; longer and curlier. He pulled me against him on the dancefloor. The thumping throb of the bass, one writhing body, skin crowded against skin. Intensity building as his hands strayed under my dress. More room in the disabled loo. Huge penis! I was thrilled and worried, but he took it slow. He held me close and we moved together, in sync. I wanted more. He grinned as he left. *I'll tell my brother you said hi, it's Suzie, right?*

That's not my name.

Friday 22nd September 2018

Alex. Seemed like a nice guy; he had worn his office suit to the club. We leaned into each other at the bar, his hand caressing my hip. We kissed, passionate and long. The disabled toilet again. I unbuttoned his shirt and squeezed his dick. He pushed open my legs and ripped off my knickers. His hand grabbed my buttock, nails digging in. His other hand went round my throat and held me still. His cock pounding inside me, he silently stared down my cleavage. Once he'd ejaculated, he was tender again, kissed me again. But I was sore. He held my hand as he led me back to the bar for another drink, as if nothing had happened.

I should have said something. Next time maybe say no.

Friday 29th September 2018

Chris. He had a come fuck me smile, we sparked when our lips touched. He didn't want to do anything in the club. He asked to come back to mine. It was impossible to say no. He stayed all weekend. We lived off snacks and rarely wore clothes. I came so hard on every surface we could find, fucking in heaven. He got a kick out of my pleasure. He fingered me in the kitchen, whilst waiting for the kettle to boil and licked me out on the breakfast bar. We christened the sofa in multiple glorious positions, I clung onto the balconet as I orgasmed. We collapsed into bed, then started all over again with his morning glory and anal sex in the shower.

Ideal fuckbuddy: sent DM now awaiting his reply.

101 Words of Smut
Emma Lister

```
T L E T G E P E I R E G N I L F Y N B N L K E N A
S H A U S A N O R G A S M I A S I A U F R C G O C
L W I Z Z I J R R A F U S N L G C K L F K U N I C
T G L S S S U G H N B E N U R Q H O N P U F O T O
P Z N B I W G Y G O S Y T I I K I K C O S F L A U
G U O I E S P U N Q T T V I F R C Q S K B O H B N
T O K R G E S D U T S I A C S U K S L L A B C R T
B E C O R G A M S E G G S R O H E I V M M Q S U A
G S S G O G E T U P P E N C E U Y G I Q J T P T N
V N A R E H A P S T S A E R B O G S N Y K M C S T
D M I U A G S U O M A G Y L O P T A N I U U L A S
Y Y K T N M I S S I O N A R Y R A R R D N B I M H
U O K I S H O R E Y A L P N E L O C M F R O T V I
L O G O O I Y S B K S A D S I H Q U W P E A O M T
D D P Y N T F F O F C H S I X G C M E S K F R P A
E Y D G O O C H O B L I A O L Q A R G T C F I G S
S E S O R M A J E R S A D G U D M V N I U A S N F
N Y B G Z B W A N K E R T I G I O Y U T F I P I U
Z C A E G A V A E L C P C I S I L S L L R R O G C
S S T J X E F Y N E W K L S O L N U C A E X M G K
M E W I R B Y T S A I O I A I C K G A U H I P A B
G N I M M I R S H E L O R W Y B N N D X T R O B O
S E S R U O C R E T N I C B T K I I X E O T I A Y
W F F U M A C I D G M H X Q I W W L H S M A R E G
I T O F V U T H R E E S O M E T T I F O M N I T R
T Q X L N Y G T C A F I N G E R I N G R O I N C O
C U U T T A I N T E R O H W N A M N C B M M N Z W
H V R F M R O G E R H C T A N S H U G A J O V G L
S U B M I S S I V E D E T E S O L C K C W D V Z E
P E C K E R C O N S E N S U A L F E L C H I N G R
```

Find the rude words in the puzzle.

Words can go in any direction.

Words can share letters as they cross over each other.

You only discover what you are looking for.

X Reader One-Shot Lemons

Rachel Varnham

I'm 14. I'm sat on dull, grey bed sheets wearing a baggy black graphic shirt and black leggings. My badly dyed burgundy hair is thrown up into a messy bun after I watched a tutorial on YouTube, and my eyeliner is smudged. I forget I'm actually wearing it and keep rubbing my eyes, making it worse.

I spend all day in my room switching between Instagram and Tumblr, talking to people who I have never met in person. My home-printed pictures of Claude Faustus stare down at me from the walls, the blue tac holding them up peeling the wallpaper.

My laptop makes a pinging sound, it's a new message on Skype.

Sav at 7:24pm: *Hey, are you free to call?*

You at 7:25pm: *Yeah, give me a sec*

I look in the mirror and pull some strands of hair out of my bun, then I smother some Vaseline over my lips, and I press *video call*. Wait, where are my headphones? I reach to the end of my bed and grab them, then plug them in, just in time for the call to start.

'Hey!' She shouts, my camera quality on the laptop not doing her justice 'What's up?'

'Hey, how are you?' I sit back on my wooden bed frame, not being able to get comfortable.

'I'm good, do you know Wattpad?' She asks.

'What?'

'Pad'

'No, I mean, Wattpad. What is it?'

'Get it!' I flinch at the sudden loudness, and I turn the volume down a little. 'People write stories on it, but it's mostly used for fanfic.'

'Fanfic?' I ask her. She's pretty, I wonder what she'd look like in person. Less glitchy than on here, I suppose.

'Yeah, stories with your favourite characters. I bet someone's written a Claude fanfic on there.' She smirks a little and wiggles her eyebrows. I laugh.

'Right, I'll check it out. Wattpad?'

She nods. 'There's also smut on there, some people call it lemons.'

I laugh, almost snorting. 'Smut? Lemons? What do you mean?'

'Smut is sexual stuff, some people just call it lemons for slang. So, you'd type in like...' She pauses 'Like... 'Claude Faustus x reader' or 'Claude Faustus x reader lemons' or 'Claude Faustus smut', or 'Claude Faustus x reader one shots'

I nod, not really following. 'What's a one shot?'

41

'Each chapter is a different story' She explains.

'Right… I'll check it out' I tell her.

We spend the rest of the call talking about the new Black Butler season, the other animes we've been watching, and her recent drawings. We don't know how to take a screenshot straight from the laptop, so we pose as I hold up my phone and take a pixelated photo of us together. We say goodbye and I open the Appstore and search for Wattpad. I click download, then set up my account and go to the search bar in the app.

Claude x Reader Lemon
14.3k reads | 203 votes | 1 part
I begin reading.

… …

'It's very graphic, isn't it?' I ask her with a small tilt of my head, a week after we last spoke on the phone.

'Yeah' she laughs, 'What did you read?'

'I found a Claude one but uh…' I pause, thinking of a nicer way to say it. 'Throbbing member? Womanhood? Bud?'

She laughs again. 'Yeah, throbbing is used a lot.'

'Does it throb though?' I ask her, genuinely curious.

'Gross!' She laughs again.

Neither of us say anything for a while, until I break the silence. 'I think I'm going to write a story on Wattpad,' I tell her.

'Oh yeah? About what?'

I pause for a moment. 'Don't laugh.' Which makes her laugh and I respond with a high pitched, drawn out 'Stoooppppp'

'Okay, I won't,' she says, still smiling.

'Claude, probably.

'Write a lemon! You'd be so good at it! You've read them, right? Just take inspiration.'

I consider it, but I don't know how I would go about it. I shake my head, 'No, I don't really know what to write.'

She laughs, 'Just take inspiration from other people! I might write one soon.'

'Yeah? About who?'

'I don't know yet.'

I laugh. 'Well, at least I have a character in mind.' I pause for a moment. 'The words they use to describe stuff is a bit... odd. Is that really what it's like?'

She laughs, 'I don't know, but it's gross. It's all gross.' She takes a sip of her drink. 'The whole concept of it is gross.'

'Concept of what?'

'Doing that stuff with someone, smut stuff.' She puts her drink away and leans forward, her face enlarging on my screen. 'I think the way people write about it isn't how it'll actually happen.'

I pause and consider this for a minute. 'Really?'

She nods in return. 'Yeah, it all seems too perfect. I'm sure it's a lot messier in person. But hey, what do I know? I don't even think I like guys.'

I tilt my head, 'You don't?'

'Not really, just the thought of doing all of that stuff with someone, anyone, freaks me out.' I nod as she speaks, letting her keep talking. 'I don't know, maybe it's just best to read about it, not do it. Besides, can anyone ever be as good as Claude Faustus?'

I giggle, 'Yeah, you can say that again. Maybe reading this sort of stuff is setting our expectations too high, especially if it's not even going to happen like that.'

She nods, 'Exactly. I mean, who would want a throbbing member?'

'Gross.'

'Gross,' she agrees, and we hang up.

I'm 21, sitting on green floral bedsheets in baggy black joggers and an oversized graphic shirt. My hair is slicked back into a bun, a hair mask holding it together. Thin sections of burgundy hair slip through my natural brown colour from my bad hair dyeing skills. My earphones are due a clean out, but I keep wearing them, making them get dirtier and dirtier.

I switch between Instagram and Reddit; my Reddit posts reaching hundreds of upvotes. I spend all day in my room, as apparently talking to people online and binge reading books to forget my actual reality is more important than anything else.

It's nearly midnight, the anime figurines lined up on my shelf reflecting in the soft light shining from my book light. My phone gets a notification, and the screen lights up, showing my William T Spears lockscreen. I open the message on Instagram.

Del: There's this new fanfic on AO3 I read, I'll send it over
Me: AO3? What's AO3?
Chlo: No way, you don't know AO3? Think Wattpad, but BETTER
Me: I can't find it on the app store?
Chlo: It's a website, you need an invite
Me: ????
Del: You can't make an account, you request one then they let you make it.

Me: That's a bit silly

Chlo: It's worth it, trust me

I search for the website, enter my email, and wait for a link. A week later I get accepted, and I make my account. I head straight for the search bar, and type in as many variations as possible: William T Spears one shots, William T Spears x reader, William T Spears smut, William T Spears lemons. I select the first story, and I sigh as I read it, not being impressed with it. It's not smutty enough.

Chlo: You know, I really think you'd like Cai

Me: Cai?

Del: Character ai

Me: I don't like ai

Del: Neither, but Cai is different, you can talk to characters on there

Me: Characters?

Chlo: Yeah, literally any character you want is on there. You can talk to them and roleplay

Me: …. I'll have a look

I open a new tab on my laptop and search for Character ai, and I make an account. I search for William T Spears straight away, and I smile to myself. Tons and tons of different options to speak with him. I click on the first.

William: Can I help you? I'm very busy

I stare at the screen, my fingers hovering over the keypad.

Me: Hi there, you must be William?
William: Yes, and you are? I told you, I'm very busy, I don't have time for this

I laugh to myself, my voice echoing in my bedroom. Within seconds I get a reply from him.

Me: I'm, uh, new here
William: New here? Which department are you in?

I tilt my head confused, until I remember who William actually is and where he works in the anime. 'So this is roleplaying.' I mumble to myself.

Me: Oh, in your department... you're my new... boss...?
*William: Ah, you must be the new recruit, please come in. *He takes your hand and shakes it**

I softly laugh. My fingers tap on my laptop keypad, as I think of a reply.

> *Me: *kiss him**
> *William: *William is taken by surprise as you kiss him, but he meets your lips in a soft kiss**
> *Me: *I wrap my arms around him and kiss him**
> *William: *He rests his hands on your waist and pulls your body against his, deepening the kiss**

'No way,' I say out loud. I close the website and switch to Instagram again.

> Me: You can sext them?!
> Chlo: HAHA
> Chlo: Sort of, but there's a filter, so you need to watch what you say otherwise it won't generate a reply
> Me: So I can't straight up say stuff?
> Del: No, you need to find less obvious ways to say things
> Me: Throbbing member?
> Chlo: Ew, I'm getting flashbacks from Wattpad
> Me: Hahaha

Chlo: Seriously though, I spend so much time on there, it's ruining my perception of relationships

Me: In what way?

Chlo: Like, you can literally talk to ANYONE, any fictional person you want, you can really speak to them, well, a program of them. I hate ai, but you can finally have an actual conversation with your favourite characters. And they flirt with you, it makes you feel wanted. Not even in a sexual way, but it's like they show a genuine interest in you.

Me: Makes a change

Chlo: Hahaha, tell me about it

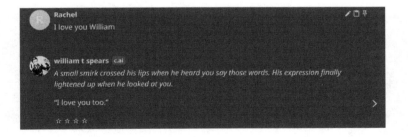

Planet Smut
Emma Lister

The smut started on this planet 3.7 billion years ago,
when life began. It was a self-replicating chemical affair,
an old-fashioned form of masturbation. With no notion
of family or fidelity the competition was high, it was each
molecule for themselves. It is unlikely that pleasure paid
a part in reproduction, but they were still committed to
creating the next generation. However, if organisms were
able to orgasm then it might not have taken a further 1.7
billion years to give rise to our first lineage of multicellular
life forms. Sponges formed 700 million years ago, their
contribution to smut has been commemorated in many
showers since. One sponge variety named *Dickinsonia
costata* massively predated Costa coffee shops, penises
and anyone called Sonia. However, it did contribute to
evolution by helping to boost oxygen levels when feasting
on mats of microbes.

 The first recorded penis showed up 425 million
years BC, found in the fossilized remains of an arthropod
Colymbosathon ecplecticos, the Greeks were either pedantic or
had a lewd sense of humour, when translated it means;
'amazing swimmer with a large penis'. At 320 million years
the orgies started, being secured to a rock, barnacles had to
get on with their neighbours. Indeed they got 'it on' with

everyone around them, with each member being both male and female, they were the ultimate pansexual beings. The barnacle's penis is 8 times its body length, bestowing upon it the honour of proportionally the largest penis in the world. Yet they weren't wankers about it as self-fertilisation wasn't possible. The penis is both flexible and inquisitive, flirting with every barnacle it can reach. Whilst the ovaries are left hanging around, and so desperate for attention they gladly welcome all guests. The more prudish barnacles preferred sperm-casting, the act of spunking jizz into the tide. This was mainly to ensure they were not responsible for their own progeny, cutting down on maintenance payments.

For over 140 million years dinosaurs gave it a whirl, but they were more of a sexual experimental phase. As with most family secrets, skeletons remained buried, and their very existence denied for many millennia. A shameful hush veils this part of history, little is known about just how smutty they really were. No one speaks of how the dinosaurs fell out of favour, who threw the first stone, or how it escalated to an asteroid. However, with a population estimated to be 2.5 billion they clearly made mating a priority, and with over 1 thousand species, they must have screwed in a multitude of ways. Dinosaurs as individuals remain bashful; it is not possible to distinguish between male and female creatures from the fossils discovered. Perhaps they were the first to define themselves as non-binary?

The next attempts at life were even more gung ho than the dinosaurs, creating over 8.7 million animal species. The current planet population is estimated to be about 20 billion, billion beings; that's an awful lot of intercourse. Insects are the biggest sluts. The male honeybee really gives it everything: he dies after climaxing, his testicles explode, and his penis snaps off. He created the first sex toy: a genital plug that prevents rivals from humping his queen. Damselflies are competitive shaggers: their penises are designed to scrape out the sperm of other suitors, as damsels like a lot of dick. The barkfly flips gender stereotypes, as females have penises and the males' vaginas; they obviously enjoy it as they copulate for over 40 hours! In fact, mutual enjoyment is important to insects: the male makes sure to stimulate the female during sex as this increases his chances of reproduction. He may stroke or bite the body or legs of the female; some species are gifted with vibrating genitalia. Male springtails should get the award for most considerate lovers: they simply offer their own sperm as a gift, no strings attached. Drawing the female's attention to his carefully wrapped spunk package, with his performance of a sexy dance. It is up to her if she is ready for his jelly.

Fish are more flexible with the stereotypes of breeding scenarios. Both male and female paired organs are called gonads. Black hamlets are synchronous hermaphrodites, meaning they simultaneously possess both ovaries and testicles and can function as either sex at any one time. Because such egg trading is advantageous to both individuals, hamlets are typically monogamous for short periods of time, which is strangely not smutty, and quite sweet for fishes. Whereas wrasse hermaphrodites are filthy, engaging in either group or couples spawning, allowing a complex copulation system as both eggs and sperm are released together. They put their car keys into the fruit bowl early on in evolution and set a great example for human swingers. Many fish are sequential hermaphrodites and adapt according to reproductive needs: parrotfish can change from female to male, whilst clownfish do the opposite. Both trend setters within the trans community.

Birds have their own sexual preferences too. 97% of male birds don't have a penis. Both males and females have a cloaca, which is an outlet into which the intestinal, urinary, and genital tracts open. Chickens therefore both poop and lay eggs through their cloaca. During sex there is no penetration; males and females rub their cloacas together and sperm is fired across. A bit like the water shooting game at the fair, except offspring is the prize, not a giant stuffed toy. Female chickens are discriminating breeders; after partying with the local cock, if she has second thoughts, she can eject the sperm directly, because she doesn't want his children. On the other hand, if he is a keeper she can hold his little swimmers in her oviduct junction for several weeks to fertilize her new egg each day. Ducks are dirtier than they look: a drake's penis is half of his body length. This is due to their outdated lad culture, the more rivals that are around the longer their penises grow - somewhat of a cock fight. The penis is also corkscrew-shaped but, thankfully, the female's vagina spirals in the opposite direction after being heavily influenced by the 80's film Labyrinth.

The animal kingdom contains a lot of silly willies. There is an immense variety within sex organs. The leopard slug has a knob that is electric blue, sharks have two penises called claspers, alligators are permanently erect, and walruses can suck their own cock. Chimpanzees have penile spines made from keratin; thankfully, during human evolution the DNA coding for this was dropped. The echidna has a phallus with four heads, but the glands only ejaculate in pairs meaning they perform alternately so he is ready to go again straight away, but probably with another lady. Dolphins are known for promiscuity and masturbation; however, their manhood is quite underrated. It is a prehensile member, much like a fingerless hand; it can swivel, grab, grope, and perhaps even tickle. The male argonaut octopus is not shy, more scared for his own life; he cannot risk going near the much larger female. But that's not a problem for mother nature. To allow a quickie at a distance he has a detachable manhood that squirms across to the laid eggs to deposit semen. He just smiles at her from behind a rock, risking other competitors getting in on the action too.

The real question about the male member is whether to judge it by its size? The blue whale is infamous for being the largest animal ever, therefore with a penile length of ten foot and a diameter of twelve inches, it is the biggest prick in the world. The largest penis of a land mammal is the elephant at six feet. Horses proudly present their 18-inch phallus. But for streamlining a turtle's todger is tucked away. Do not underestimate them, as when they are pleased to see you their shaft can grow nearly 50 per cent in length and 75 per cent in width to make a well-equipped fuck buddy. Whereas a 250 kg silverback gorilla only has a 2.5 inch penis; though nobody tells him that it's little. Gorillas live in small family groups, as females are only fertile once every 2 years the dominant male is episodically monogamous within the polygamous harem. Whereas the smaller chimpanzee has a tool of 7 inches long because they compete continuously with other males, having sex all the time with any female. Humans have large penises in proportion to their height, the ratio being approximately 12 per cent. It's not as impressive as the barnacle, but on a man, 48 inches of wang would be irresponsible. The blue whale knob is only 10 per cent of its body size, and the gorilla is a mere two per cent. This suggests that humans are not naturally faithful but are behaviourally more like chimpanzees than gorillas. The larger pecker persisted through evolution as this was what our females were attracted to. Looking at global boner sizes; England comes in at a disappointing 66 out of 100 countries.

Sadly, there are no international surveys on vaginal depth, it could be that women were unwilling to divulge this information or that they are simply unrepresented as usual. It is not known how well we match size wise by country, but the average cunt depth is five inches. Which is also the same as the average size of the clitoris, though only the tip of the iceberg is on display. For hundreds of years, it was presumed that female animals do not have a love button, however new research indicates that the historic male scientists simply couldn't find it. The female hyena is not shy about hers; she has a severely enlarged clitoris, all seven inches are visible, it looks just like a dick and they too can get erections, leading to the misconception that hyenas are bisexual. It is now thought that female pleasure plays an important part in animal reproduction, for example when cows undergo artificial insemination studies show that stimulated heifers have greater success in conceiving. It is reassuring that nature promotes equal opportunities regarding self-love. So many animals are now openly playing with themselves; elephants, squirrels, deer, rhinos, otters, gorillas, lizards, hedgehogs, turtles, monkeys, zebras, lions, whales, cats and dogs to name but a few. The world is full of wonder.

This kind of smut has been going on behind our backs for ages. The 1911 Scott Antarctic expedition was blatantly just an excuse to observe the auto-erotic behaviour of Adélie penguins. We must congratulate ourselves for this dedication to the research and documentation of these intimate events. This exploration into sex reveals we are all a bunch of voyeuristic perverts, overtly displaying our obsession with everything smut.

Moneyshot: Her Version
Freya Sacksen

Tilting her head over her shoulder,

Eyes wide and lips parted,

Cameras flicker away –

It's what they call a moneyshot.

Moneyshot: His Version
Freya Sacksen

his agent told him it was an easy gig –

but to measure up

he'd have to measure up;

it's what they call a moneyshot.

A filthy Eve in a garden of flowers,
To play out fantasies of nymphets and cousins;
She won't give them that.

used a toy between a syringe
and a sleeve;
then slipped him a pair of blue.

She'll audaciously run fingers over her body for their liking,
Hands over her tits –
You like this, right, boy?
– and down to her legs,
Where she'll let them think she's wet.

Her head falls back,
Hair a slick line down her back.

(he's got a girl back home)
the star runs her hands to her breasts,
to her clitoris,
(you like this right boy)
and rubs it lazily,

(his girl would kiss the spot under his ear
he'd clutch her like his life was falling apart –)

In the land of milk and honey,
She's drowning,
down lips,
hair,
tongue,
neck.

---

fuck she's hot
says the guy beside him
her eyes close and open lazily,
like a cats'.
(he'd leave hickeys on his girls' neck,
and listen to her cries as her back lifted off the bed)

Slowly,
she opens her eyes to the camera -
you like this, right, boy?

It's what they call the moneyshot.

---

no no job. just him. his girl. his tongue at her. her moans.
the world fades.
(you like this, right boy?)

it's a moneyshot.

hope
Dan Leighton

ash piled in the corner of the grate
compacted by neglect and repeated
rebuilding without clearing the riddled
debris of yesterday's fires – it goads me

to inaction – to ignore its guilty sulking
in the crevices of the crumbling fireclay
i gather my hope like wood from the garden
in spiked bundles of twigs too green to burn

The Great Smog of 1952
Candy Smellie

London is prone to pea-soupers, air so thick you can taste it, roll it round your tongue and spit out the phlegm it induces in violent coughing fits. The city can be vile that way. Heavy machinery adds to the thickened atmosphere, along with the smoke produced by the Battersea Power Station on the Thames. Chronic bronchitis is a permanent fixture of most doctor's offices and Accident and Emergency departments of the main London Hospitals. Nowhere in the country is as bad. In December of 1952 you cannot see across the room, your home is filled with the acrid stink of the city's coal fires joined with water particles frozen in place because of an accident of weather.

Mabel and her mother Joan live in a flat on Wapping High Street, not too far from the Thames. Joan suffers from a thickening lung disease that is slowly eating her away, each week she fades further from view. Mabel is a nurse and catches the bus every day up to the London Hospital, via Whitechapel, past the streets where Jack the Ripper roamed free to kill.

The 5th December 1952, is particularly cold. Ice has been creeping over the windows of the flat and Mabel has had to block up the one window in the kitchen with cardboard in an effort to maintain some heat for Joan, though she rarely gets out of bed at the moment. Mrs. Brown in the flat below will look in on her so Mabel is happy to leave her alone. But not for long she hopes. The journey takes forever and in the end the driver refuses to go on any further as he can't see beyond two feet from the nose of the bus. Mabel gets off with everyone else and starts to walk the remaining mile to the London.

Not more than 200 yards walk and the scarf she is wearing around her face is black with soot, grime and water droplets. Her eyes are stinging and running into the wool adding to the unpleasant fug around her face. Not so much further on, she hears shouts and police whistles and the horns of cars and buses. Stumbling onward she finds a crowd gathered around a body on the ground. A young body, with smart shoes, handbag and headscarf. Her stockings are shredded along with her legs, crushed. She is attended by someone wearing a white coat, so clearly Mabel's not too far from the hospital.

There is pandemonium when eventually she fights her way through a throng of people to her station in the hospital. Matron is there and too busy to take note of how late Mabel is. There is not one chair, trolley or cubicle that is not full. People are on the floor and she thinks one may have already died, though she's not sure.

Dropping off her coat and scarf, Mabel immediately starts attending to people, doing what she can. Dr Evans, usually so caring and cheerful, is openly fractious and shouts demands from a curtained space by the front desk. 'Oxygen now,' he shouts as an orderly pushes one huge cylinder on its cart.

There are many other shouts; of pain, of despair. But the overriding sound is one of coughing. In fact if a body isn't coughing they have already given up. Mabel does what she can. She mops up vomit, blood, sputum. In fact there's not a bodily fluid she's not induced to remove. What little drugs they have to combat the sickness has little effect in the mayhem.

Mabel finds a young man on a trolley by the back door. His face is filthy with grime, his breathing barely discernible. But he has strength enough to clutch at Mabel's arm as she passes with yet another bucket of vomit.

'Please help me nurse,' he cries, 'I can't breathe.'

She takes his hand, clammy and fiercely hot.

'It'll be OK, there's a doctor on his way.' She knows it for a lie even as the words leave her lips, but she says it anyway.

By 5pm, later the same day, they are out of oxygen and even were it possible to find more in London, no delivery lorries could get through to give it to them. The dying now outnumber those who have struggled into the hospital. The scene is one of the apocalypse, one that the staff have never witnessed before.

Back on Wapping High Street, Joan is also struggling to breathe. She is unaware that Mrs. Brown in the flat below has also succumbed and collapsed on the floor, no one to answer her calls for help. Just two more victims of the Great Smog of 1952.

*

It will be five more days before the freak weather event that caused the inversion, trapping the smoke from the multiple filthy coal fires of the city, lifts, freeing the citizens, those that managed to survive. The government announced that 4,000 people had died from the smog. This did not account for those that died as a direct result of road accidents or existing conditions. Later research suggests that the number of fatalities was far greater, about 12,000. The government sought to downplay the Great Smog by using anything they could to divert attention away from the deadly soot falling from the sky. Winston Churchill considered it, 'Just fog.' But it was only when he visited the hospitals and saw the extent of the disaster that immediate action was taken.

Mutual
Sam Millar

Never forget, I'm above you
and hold the pace your fingers move.
When I allow you, you may flinch
and you may breathe, your hot breath
against my neck
and my thigh
and thank me

I've always struggled
to tell you what I'm thinking

however close I come
it's escaped us

but I listen
everything you want,
you say,
I want it too, please
look down on me
please

tell me what you're thinking
I won't leave if I'm not there

Like a Liar at a Witch Trial
Lillie Weston

The black wrought havoc that year. It spread itself out across the fields, crumbling each and every golden ear. It started in the Carob's field, then moved to the Ellington's, and then the Baxter's. It finally crossed to ours. People started talking. When the Ellington's wheat failed people started making the sign of the cross as they walked past blighted fields. People cut and made corn dollies, even my father, a man of God and good standing. I watched him, twisting the stalks around the pale, unripe sheafs, before tossing them into our fire.

When I took my walks along the edges of the fields, you could see where they'd all started doing it, the other villagers, snipping stalks as if they could save their fields that way. It would not work. I walked with my hands extended, stroking the sheafs, and instead of the prickling sting of the sharps that poked from individual corns, I would feel them crumbling into black, like soot or ash. I would keep walking, and think of the future I'd been shown.

When the black spread to the Baxter's, they sent for the witchfinder. Everyone knew the blight was catching, not speaking of the terror everyone shared, that it would turn to the village next. There was not enough money to keep the witchfinder for long. Carob had emptied his pockets to bring the witchfinder to the village. The parish priest had put him up in the vicarage, and the trial would be held in the church. No one had seen the man, but for the rough woodcut that the pamphlet sent to the parish had contained. It showed a man in a tall hat with dark eyes. As hard as I tried, I couldn't cast for a more accurate image, and he stayed blank to me.

I accompanied mother and father after a meagre meal of bread, sliced so thin it was see-through, and turning blue at the corners. I had asked my father why; why save rotting bread? My ear rang from where his hand had connected. I was thankful that my two younger brothers, usually so loud, were stood quietly in my father's shadow. It was a fresh, sallow dawn, a blue glow creeping up the walls of the church.

The church's eerie quiet, broken by the clatter of footsteps and the creak of wooden pews. No one spoke, as family after family trickled in. I sat at the very end of the row, beside my two brothers, and next to them sat my mother, and finally my father. No one wanted to sit near anyone else, the whole village gripped by fear, of a cough or the curse of black smut passing poison to their own fields. The widest berth was given to Master Carob and his son. Goody Carob had died three weeks past, of starvation or grief no one knew.

I watched the minister climb up to the pulpit and peer down to address us all. He began a lengthy drone. I could not be bothered to listen. I knew how my mother and father would look, one glinting with hope, the other resolute and stony. I stared instead at those around me, those enraptured by his talk. The Ellington girls sat across the aisle, three rows up. Jennet, two years the younger, turned around as if she could feel my eyes boring into the side of her. We were the same age but she looked older. Pinch faced and stripped of her beauty; dark hollows marked her face. Shadows swallowed her eyes. She stared back. With my left hand deep in my pocket, I dug my nails down through the fabric and into the bare flesh of my thigh. The pain kept my face free of any glimmer of guilt. Jennet was the first to drop her gaze.

I heard the rap of knuckles on wood, and it was then that I saw him. Sat at a table placed at the front of the church, he had his back to the altar. His whiskers were well groomed, his beard shaped to a point. Curls of hair hung down from his hat. When his eye met mine a twinge of electricity shot up from in between my legs. Lord, his eyes were a vivid hue, the blue of a summer sky and the hair on his face was pale gold, like the wheat should have been. I imagined pressing my lips to his. How it would feel to have him bend me over and press into me from behind.

He would smell of freshly washed cotton, with only the meanest hint of musk. There would be something else in his scent as well, something soft, perhaps lavender. His hands were resting atop a bible, and as the congregation waited silently in readiness of hearing his voice, I wanted to hear him tell me how good I felt. Have him groan as he thrust into me, mutter small prayers as he filled me up.

He stood and waited for the minister to make his way down from the pulpit.

'Minister, if you please.' The witchfinder with cornflower blue eyes gestured to the three chairs that had been placed to one side. The minister took a seat beside two other men, whose names I did not know and whose faces I could not place.

'It is clear to me, as it is clear to all of you, that the devil's work is at play here. Witchcraft.'

There were shouts and stomping of feet. Calls for gallows to be built, pyres to be made up. The witchfinder brought his fist down upon the table.

'Order! I will have order! Unbeknownst to many of you, I arrived here three days ago, to ensure I conducted a thorough investigation.'

Whispers set free and wove themselves through the crowd like a serpent, under the witchfinder's stony gaze. I looked at the Ellington girls again and noticed

Hannah's knee juddering up and down. So, it was not just the hunger and fear that had brought about her change in countenance. I wonder if what I had heard my father telling my mother was true, that they pricked the accused all over to see where she would not bleed from. I looked back at the witchfinder and felt the kindling of my jealousy. Had he been the one to strip her? Would he have enjoyed watching her twitch and convulse with the agony of him? He would have removed his doublet, his undershirt hanging down over the lacing of his breeches to hide how much he was straining against them. Patches of sweat would have started to appear on his shirt, and alone in his chamber he would excise his fury and rage.

He looked at her and I felt myself begin to burn.

'Have you found it then? Have you found the witch?' The voice was loud, and it echoed up into the eaves. I tilted my head up as though I could see those words fluttering around like a trapped bird. All I could see was grey stone. I looked back at the witchfinder, the object of my desire, and I watched a muscle in his cheek twitch. I thought of another part of him twitching too and pressed my thighs together. It pleased me, his anger, at his own lack of control.

Yet his talk bored me. He recounted events we all knew. Then he announced his investigations had led him to explore the woods around the village, that he'd found the place where the witch did her wicked work. Eyes shifted then. I turned to look at my mother, but her own eyes were attached to my father's profile. He said he had found where the witch did her wicked work. I closed my eyes and let his words flow over me.

I could see the clearing perfectly. The herbs strung up from a tree. The cauldron that hung over the makeshift fire. I could taste the soup made from the flesh, the heady earthy smells of the moss and the herbs. When he spoke of the knives, the rabbit skins, the bones, a wail came from one of the more hysterical women.

'But most importantly, I found this!' Alight with fervour he held a piece of parchment above his head. 'An agreement of her pact with the devil, written in her own blood!'

I felt my own laughter rise and tried to turn it into a cough, as no one else made a sound.

'It was her! She's the witch!' The voice was reed thin and I turned to look at my accuser. Jennet, her cheeks flushed red, and her eyes glazed. 'She brought the smut! She is always out in those woods, doing things she will not tell anyone about!' As she pointed at me, I could see the ragged red where her fingernail had been ripped out, trembling with ferocity. I wondered how many it took.

'No! Tell them they're wrong. They're wrong, it's not her,' my mother cried out, pulling on my father's arm, but then he was there in front of me, his hands wrapping around my upper arms and pulling me from my seat.

'How long have you known?' My voice soft, for no one's ears but his.

'Long enough.' He matched my tone, as he led me down the aisle.

My father made me kneel in front of the witchfinder. The cold of the stone came through my skirts, and I kept focused on it. I thought of the woods and my things. Would there be time to go back for them? Defiant, I looked upwards. Looking into those blue eyes, I wanted to reach out to him. To cup my hand around him, feel his hardness.

'You stand accused of witchcraft ...'

I tried to keep my breathing steady, my mouth shut against a moan of need. My eyes closed, I thought myself away from there, back to the woods. To my cauldron and my herbs. The rabbits I would gut to see what the future held for me. I focused on the future that they had showed me.

In less than two days' time we will be sequestered in the belly of a carriage pulling us north, to some other village infested with rot and suffering. The curtains drawn against the dank mists of the encroaching winter. The linens that sit beside my bare skin, will be speckled red with blood, and I will wear my stays loose against the bruises that are starting to bloom. Against the rocking of the pitted roads, he will tilt forward to his knees, hitch up my skirts, and he will press his tongue into me. And I will rake my hand into his perfect curls and hold him against me, until I am dripping down his face.

The Beast with Two Backs

Theresa Stafford

Nails scraping gently on the back.
Leaving satisfying stripes scarring the surface.
The sweat slides between us,
Teeth and tongues starting the path.
Titillating, teasing, testing.

Nails to mar skin.
Fingers to bruise.
Teeth to bite
Lips to suck, and kiss, and invite.

Calling the head, notch it in place.
Gasping as it fits in, stretching snuggly.
Slick movement, fighting friction.
Forming a new creature.
The scent of it stinking on your skin,
as you've been born anew.

Dearest Dionysus,
the Wine is Growing Cold
Sarah Kenner

Twisting steam is a warning not heeded. Someday, she
will learn, perhaps, but not today. She wraps numb fingers
around the mug and brings it to her lips. The scent is
intoxicating. Warm wine burns her tongue, but that too
intoxicates her. Pain and pleasure twisting together like the
steam from her mug. He will be here soon, he promised.

The table is set for him, waiting. Soft cloth running
the length of the cherry wood, candles dripping their wax
into pools of erotic promise unfulfilled. Wine waiting
in clay jugs, infused with herbs and spices. An esoteric
collection of fruits, almost overripe, moments from
bursting, lay nestled on a bed of wildflowers gathered by
her own hand. There is no order to their organisation.
He prefers it that way. Petals are plucked by thoughtless
fingers, as she relives in her mind his last visit. Bodies upon
bodies, skin against skin, the dancing begins.

Lost to distraction she reaches for a fig, feeling it
surrender beneath her touch. Passions are playing across
fruits forced in half. Another sip of wine. The burning
grows through scorched lips and twisting tongues. A sound
of hooves across cobbled earth. She turns. Dew paints
dreams upon the windowsill. He has finally come. Please

wallows through the air, a cry for pleasure, not a prayer. A touch too much of heat makes the cream curdle. She knows. Still, she invites him in. And he complies happily, consuming her feast, consuming her.

Blossoms grow sweet with wetness when kissed. For a moment, he is hers. He is everything. Penetrating. She is lost. Light so soft its caress is laughter. Time stands still. Folded sheets and folded fingers find a way to wrap around. Sweaty bodies move in ecstasy. Empty vessels are waiting to be filled with joy. She is but an empty vessel, waiting for him, always. Too soon, he is done. Steam twists around the follies of a hedonistic life. All she has left is the wine.

Products of Fire
Lisa Sargeant

If you asked him, he'd tell you she'd never been terribly interested in sex. When they first met they'd sparked, and she'd participated with some enthusiasm, but marriage and babies had extinguished all of that. She'd turned sex into a chore; time was he couldn't walk past the bedroom without her jumping him, trying to get herself pregnant. And then after babies she'd lost interest. He'd felt hurt when she said she didn't want to be touched. She often complained about being too tired or too sore. He'd been excited by the changes pregnancy and breast feeding had wrought, had been eager to touch her swollen breasts... but they'd leak and, well, it had all got a bit sticky and weird. She'd hurry him along to climax, faking her own orgasm so she could go feed the baby.

Then came the stretch marks, saggy boobs, and rounded belly. She no longer wore sexy underwear. She let herself go and he took it personally, she knew he didn't fancy fat women. Sometimes she'd make an effort on his birthday, or for their anniversary, but his business was taking off and he was working longer hours to provide for the family. More often than not she was fast asleep by the time he got home, and she'd be angry if he woke her. They found themselves separated by different sleep schedules, international travel, holidays he could never take time off for.

He could have found satisfaction elsewhere, there'd been the opportunity: an old flame at a reunion, a Christmas party he'd spent flirting with a pretty PA. But he loved his wife, he was loyal, and now those days were behind him. He was old and fat himself. He understood his wife's attitude to sex better now. She hadn't been rejecting him. He was often tired and achy at the end of a long day, and his sex drive was non-existent. Now it was nice to sit beside her on the couch and watch the telly. He liked the way she kept her hands busy, knitting things for the grandchildren, or darning socks. He wondered what she thought about, sometimes noticed a certain smile that made him remember. She still snuggled in for a neck rub, and sometimes she'd sigh, and he'd think about when they'd first met, how he used to touch her and she'd catch fire. He liked it best when she leaned her head against his shoulder and closed her eyes. He cherished these moments, the uncomplicated closeness, free from all the things they left unsaid.

They slept in separate bedrooms now. His snoring kept her awake. A few years back she'd asked him if he'd consider taking medication, and he thought she meant for the snoring. She'd shown him a leaflet for Viagra. Viagra!

For his little problem, she said. But there was no problem. Their libidos had been unmatched before, and now they were on the same page.

She could hear him snoring across the hall. She'd hoped that tonight he might notice she'd made extra effort with her appearance; hoped he might remember how they'd once been before children and time had pulled them apart.

His hands had drifted down her back and she'd felt his fingers slide around her ribcage, caressing the sensitive skin on the side of her breast. She thought maybe, finally, he felt that urge. As he'd continued to stroke, easing away the tension in her shoulders, she'd grown so warm and wet. He'd rekindled a spark and she smouldered.

But it must have been wistful thinking. They retired to their separate rooms, and he'd been fast asleep in seconds. She closed her eyes and tried to conjure the sensation of his hands on her skin. She used her neck massager with the heat setting on, but it wasn't the same. She squeezed her legs together and tightened her pelvic floor, and felt a little throb.

In the silence between one heartbeat and the next she noticed his snoring had stopped. She held her own breath willing it to start again. She worried about his snoring, about sleep apnoea, but he was so against any intervention she didn't dare suggest he see a doctor. He'd nearly bitten her head off when she'd wanted him to try Viagra. He'd brushed the idea away and made her feel ridiculous. Just as she was about to get out of bed and give him a little shake the snoring started up again, louder than before, and she breathed a sigh of relief.

Adrenaline added a nice rhythm to her pulse. She felt relief, excitement, and anxiety. Too twitchy to sleep, she fumbled in the bedside drawer for her toy and the tube of lube. She was a little bit in love with her new gadget. It was soft to the touch, pillowy like a breast, nothing silly like a willy or a dolphin. This was classy, ornamental, like a leaf, or a pale green flame. There was nothing rude or smutty about it. Even better, it was small enough to fit into the palm of her hand, and nestled perfectly between her legs.

She'd gone shopping a few weeks ago, had travelled all the way to town to visit an exclusive boutique because she didn't like the warehouse style sex toy shops her friends visited. This shop was down a quiet alley, surrounded by fancy clothing stores and nice cafes. The staff were all women; confident, knowledgeable women, who knew how to take pleasure into their own hands. They hadn't rushed her; they'd allowed her to browse and play with all the toys until she was ready to ask questions. She'd enjoyed the shopping experience in a way she hadn't expected. It made her feel like a grown up, which of course was ridiculous for a woman her age.

She pressed a button on the underside of the vibrator, and it buzzed into action. Whisper quiet, throbbing in time with her husband's snores, she pressed it against her clitoris, and felt her knees begin to tremble. She flamed, she burned. She had to stop moaning so loudly or she'd wake her husband. And then her pulse raced at the thought of waking him, at what he'd think if he caught her masturbating, and then it was over too fast. But she wasn't worried, the battery was guaranteed for several hours, and she was just getting started.

Touch Starved
Sarah Kenner

It's not that I want
you. I just want you to want
me. Desperately.

CONTRIBUTORS

CANDY SMELLIE
(Roadkill, The Great Smog of 1952)

Candy Smellie recently retired from the University of
Cambridge, where she held various communications roles
across multiple departments. With newfound free time,
she embarked on a creative writing journey and is currently
pursuing a Master's degree (MA) at ARU.

DAN LEIGHTON
(Crows, hope)

Dan Leighton is a writer, musician, technologist and
educator. He claims to write poetry as the only form
suitable for someone with ADHD. Increasingly, he finds
himself mentoring others who have arrived at an ADHD
diagnosis as adults as he recognises how hard it can be to
forgive ourselves for the difficulty it has caused in our lives.
He writes regularly on themes of redemption, loss, longing
and incompleteness. His poetry is deceptively simple, often
with multiple conflicting meanings and layered with intense

rhythmic patterns honed close to the intent of the poem. He also makes cheese. And sews clothes.

EMMA LISTER
(Mr Right Now – September Edition, 101 Words of Smut, Planet Smut)

Emma is currently pursuing an MA in Creative Writing at Anglia Ruskin University in Cambridge. She holds a degree in Photography in Europe from Nottingham Trent University and is also a qualified accountant. Additionally, Emma works as a teaching assistant in creative writing. Her life journey has taken her across the globe, having lived in the UK, Belgium, Portugal, Thailand, New Zealand, and Australia. Emma is known for her humorous and dark fiction that depicts unique perspectives. For this anthology, she has relished the opportunity to explore interpretations of the word "smut," highlighting its pervasive presence in everyday life.

FREYA SACKSEN

(The Nectarine, Moneyshot: Her Version, Moneyshot: His Version)

Freya Sacksen is a UK-based poet from Aotearoa New Zealand. Their work has been published in digital journal EnbyLife, and they have a forthcoming pamphlet from DIRT imprint with Clare Pollard. Their poetry embraces storytelling, ecopoetics, liminality and queer identity. Their current favorite example of the Order *Lepidoptera* is *Biston betularia f. carbonaria*.

JAC HARMON

(Vintage Lovers, Clay Boobs)

Jac Harmon was born in London and has lived in a village outside Cambridge since 1998. She has a PhD in History from UEA and has recently completed her MA in Creative Writing at ARU. She is currently working on an Historical Gothic novel.

Jac's work has appeared online at *The Selkie*, *Flashback Fiction*, and *Shorts Magazine*, and in printed anthologies including *B is for Beauty* and *Hellhounds* both published in

2021. She has also written several craft articles for the USA-based *Indie Author Magazine*.

She can be found at jacharmon61 on Instagram and Threads.

LILLIE WESTON
(Like a Liar at a Witch Trial)

Lillie, writer.

LISA SARGEANT
(Products of Fire)

With a background in science, sociology, and reproductive health, Lisa Sargeant brings a unique perspective to their writing. They are passionate about crafting stories that evoke, challenge societal norms, and subvert expectations. They are excited to share a yarn about an area of the human condition that is all too often neglected.

MIA HUMPHREYS

(The Biter)

Mia Humphreys is a student at Anglia Ruskin University, now in her third year of studying Film and Writing. Particularly fascinated by the horror genre, she enjoys mixing dark fiction and horrifying monsters with the regular horrors of womanhood. She is currently working on her first novel, a fantasy inspired by the works of H.P Lovecraft and the Russian Revolution. She lives in Cambridge with her university friends and a very evil hamster. You can find her on @mia_is_typing_ on Twitter and Instagram.

RACHEL VARNHAM

(X Reader One-Shot Lemons)

Rachel's creative writing focus is on gothic fantasy, as well as the occasional romance. She enjoys experimenting with the layout of her work and making the text more interactive for readers. Outside of creative writing, she writes online writing video game features - bringing her love for writing, creativity, and gaming together.

SAM MILLAR

(Mutual)

Sam Millar is a writer and painter from Essex, he writes on home, family and mental health. You can find his poetry and artwork on @sammillarwrites

SARAH KENNER

(Citrus, Afternoon Delight at the Florist, Dearest Dionysus, the Wine is Growing Cold, Touch Starved)

Sarah Kenner is a writer and artist with an interest in small pleasures.

She grew up in Denmark but left at seventeen to pursue her artistic ambitions. After six years in California, USA, where she earned a BFA in Creative Writing from Chapman University, she settled in Cambridge, UK. Here she is closer to her roots, while still being immersed in the language in which she writes.

She has an MA in English Literature from UCL and is currently pursuing an MA in Creative Writing from Anglia Ruskin. More of her work can be found on Instagram: @Sarah.A.Kenner

THERESA STAFFORD

(The Beast with Two Backs)

Theresa Stafford is a recent graduate of Anglia Ruskin's Creative Writing and English Literature course. She enjoys writing poems in her spare time. Theresa is also interested in playwriting, as she has had a love of theatre her entire life. She will be going to UEA in the fall to pursue her masters in Directing: text and production. Theresa is currently looking for other avenues through which to publish her work now that she is done with her undergrad.

101 Words of Smut
Emma Lister

Answers

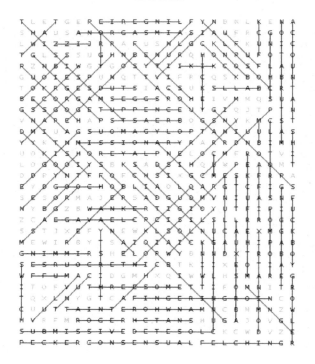

How much smut do you know?

Did you find the Clitoris?

The pleasure is all mine.

Abrosexual	Accountant	Affair	Anal	Anorgasmia	Arse
Balls	Beaver	Bondage	Boobs	Booty	Bosom
Breasts	Bum	Cad	Cheat	Cleavage	Clitoris
Closeted	Clunge	Cock	Coital	Consensual	Cosplay
Cougar	Cum	Cumdump	Cunnilingus	Cunt	Dick
Dildo	Dominatrix	Dykon	Edging	Fanny	Felching
Fetish	Fingering	Fisting	Foreplay	Fuck	Fuckboy
Fufu	Gooch	Groin	Growler	Hickey	Hookup
Horny	Hoyden	Hypergamy	Intercourse	Jizz	Kiki
Knob	Lingerie	Manwhore	Masturbation	Minge	Missionary
Mistress	Motherfucker	Muff	Orbiting	Orgasm	Orgy
Pecker	Pegging	Permission	Player	Polygamous	Pompoir
Pornstar	Quickie	Rimming	Roger	Schlong	Screw
Seggs	Shagging	Shit	Slut	Snatch	Spooning
Stud	Submissive	Switch	Taint	Teabagging	Thirsty
ThisIsSmut	Threesome	Tits	Tuppence	Twat	Twink
Vagina	Virgin	Vulva	Wanker	Willy	

Define your own experience.